GW00706045

Where *Love* REIGNS

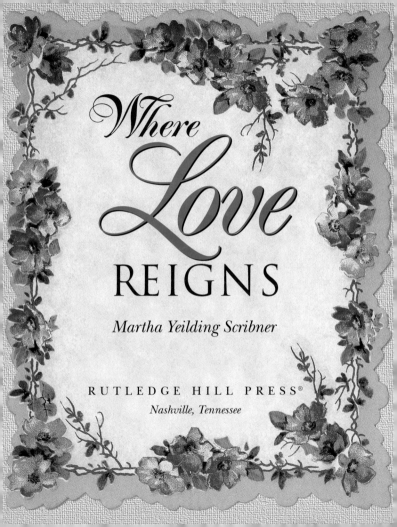

Where *Love* REIGNS

Martha Yeilding Scribner

RUTLEDGE HILL PRESS®

Nashville, Tennessee

Published by Rutledge Hill Press®, Inc.,
211 Seventh Avenue North, Nashville, Tennessee 37219.
Distributed in Canada by H. B. Fenn & Company, Ltd.,
34 Nixon Road, Bolton, Ontario L7E 1W2.
Distributed in Australia by Five Mile Press Pty, Ltd.,
22 Summit Road, Noble Park, Victoria 3174.
Distributed in New Zealand by Tandem Press,
2 Rugby Road, Birkenhead, Auckland 10.
Distributed in the United Kingdom by Verulam Publishing, Ltd.,
152a Park Street Lane, Park Street, St. Albans, Hertfordshire AL2 2AU.

Design & composition by Gore Studio Inc.

Library of Congress Cataloging-in-Publication Data

Where love reigns / [compiled] by Martha Yeilding Scribner.
        p.   cm.
    ISBN 1-55853-671-X (hardbound)
    1. Love—Quotations, maxims, etc.   2. Quotations, English.
I. Scribner, Martha Yeilding, 1964–
PN6084.L6W425   1998
820.8'03543—dc21   98-36680
                                                                   CIP

Printed in the United States of America

1 2 3 4 5 6 7 8 9—02 01 00 99 98

INTRODUCTION

How do I love thee? Let me count the ways…

These simple lines, written by Elizabeth Barrett Browning, are some of the most touching words ever written. Love—that elusive, dynamic, fickle, wonderful emotion—means something different to each person. We are fascinated by love, and each of us tries to describe it, understand it, and capture it in our own way.

The mystery of love is ageless. Every era of history has its own concept of what True

Love is, from the earliest words inscribed on the walls of Egyptian tombs to the ancient wisdom of the Bible; from the medieval codes of chivalry to the great Victorian poets and modern novelists.

Through the centuries, poets and writers have given us some of the most memorable words about love. Sometimes they seem to understand the nature of love better than we ourselves, and their words inspire us to contemplate our own loves, whether we have won or lost them. They inspire us to love again, always in search of the mystery of True Love.

Collected here are some familiar and some not-so-familiar expressions of love

from the Victorian era. Because their true-life love story is so touching, the words of Elizabeth Barrett and Robert Browning have inspired lovers all over the world. In January of 1845 Robert Browning read his own name in one of Elizabeth's poems. He wrote her, "I do...love these books with all my heart—and I love you too." They courted through letters, and Elizabeth's passion inspired her to write *Sonnets from the Portuguese.* The couple met face-to-face the next May, and, because her father did not approve of their love affair, they eloped to Florence, Italy, to marry. The lived in Florence for fifteen years, and they continued to express their love in poetry and correspondence, giving us some of the most poignant words of love ever written.

The Brownings and their contemporaries invite us to feel the passion or pain, the tenderness or tension, the honesty or hopelessness that love brings to us all. We realize, as all lovers before us have realized, that it is "better to have loved and lost, than never to have loved at all."

Where
Love
REIGNS

How do I love thee? Let me count the ways.
I love thee to the depth and breadth and height
My soul can reach, when feeling out of sight
For the ends of Being and ideal Grace.
I love thee to the level of everyday's
Most quiet need, by sun and candle-light.
I love thee freely, as men strive for Right;
I love thee purely, as they turn from Praise.
I love thee with the passion put to use
In my old griefs, and with my childhood's faith.
I love thee with a love I seemed to lose
With my lost saints,—I love thee with the breath,
Smiles, tears, of all my life!—and, if God choose,
I shall but love thee better after death.

—*Elizabeth Barrett Browning*

I chose my wife, as she did her wedding gown, not for a fine glossy surface, but such qualities as would wear well.

—*Oliver Goldsmith*

The simple lack of her is more to me than others' presence.

—*Edward Thomas*

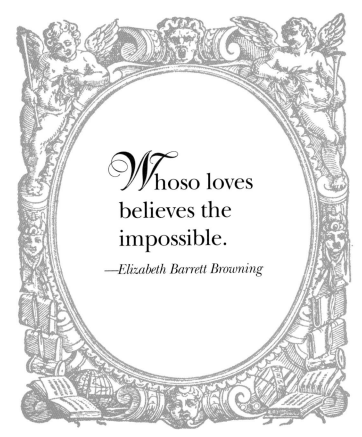

Whoso loves
believes the
impossible.

—*Elizabeth Barrett Browning*

THE AUTHORESS
by Grace Aguilar

---

*I*t is no shame now, dear Granville, to confess how deeply and constantly I have returned your affection; but listen to me, ere you proceed further. I do not doubt what you say, that your prejudices are all removed; but are you certain, quite certain, that a woman who has resources of mind as well as of heart can make you happy, as you believe? At one-and-twenty you could have molded me to what you pleased. I doubt whether I should have written another line, had you not approved of my doing it. At one-and-thirty this cannot be. My character—my habits are formed. I cannot draw back from my literary path, for I feel it accomplished good. Can I indeed make your happiness as I am? Dearest Granville, do not let feeling alone decide."

"Feeling! Sense! Reason! Clara—my own Clara—all speak and have spoken long. Make my child but like yourself, and with two such blessings I dare not picture what life would be—too, too much joy.

*G*ive all to love;
Obey thy heart;
Friends, kindred, days,
Estate, good fame,
Plans, credit and the Muse,
Nothing refuse.

—*Ralph Waldo Emerson*

A lover without indiscretion
is no lover at all.

—*Thomas Hardy*

*T*he birthday of my life
Is come, my love is come to me.

—*Christina Rossetti*

*N*ever the time and the place
And the loved one all together!

—*Robert Browning*

*O*h heart! Oh blood that freezes, blood that burns!
Earth's returns
For whole centuries of folly, noise and sin!
Shut them in,
With their triumphs and their glories and the rest!
Love is best!

—*Robert Browning*

*L*ove is the state in which man sees things most widely different from what they are. The force of illusion reaches its zenith here, as likewise the sweetening and transfiguring power. When a man is in love he endures more than at other times; he submits to everything.

—*Friedrich Nietzsche*

My heart is like a singing bird
Whose nest is in a watered shoot:
My heart is like an apple tree
Whose boughs are bent with
	thickset fruit;
My heart is like a rainbow shell
That paddles in a halcyon sea;
My heart is gladder than all these
Because my love is come to me.

—*Christina Rossetti*

The delight that consumes the desire,
The desire that outruns the delight.

—*Algernon Charles Swinburne*

How good is man's life, the mere
living! how fit to employ
All the heart and the soul and the senses
forever in joy!

—*Robert Browning*

"DE AMICITIA"
by Somerset Maugham

They stood side by side, leaning against the parapet, looking down at the water.…And from the water rose up Love, and Love fluttered down from the trees, and Love was borne along upon the night air. Ferdinand did not know what was happening to him; he felt Valentia by his side, and he drew closer to her, till her dress touched his legs and the silk of her sleeve rubbed against his arm. It was so dark that he could not see her face; he wondered of what she was thinking. She made a little movement and to him came a faint wave of the scent she wore. Presently two forms passed by on the bank and they saw a lover with his arm round a girl's waist, and

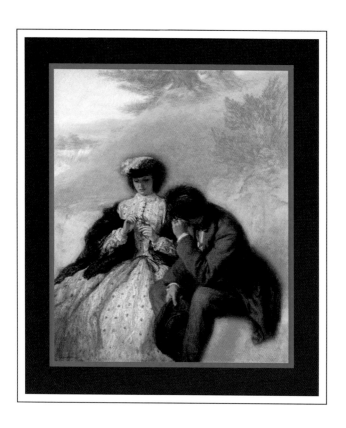

then they too were hidden in the darkness. Ferdinand trembled as he spoke.

"Only Love is waking!"

"And we!" she said.

"And—you!"

He wondered why she said nothing. Did she understand? He put his hand on her arm.

"Valentia!"

He had never called her by her Christian name before. She turned her face towards him.

"What do you mean?"

"Oh, Valentia, I love you! I can't help it."

A sob burst from her.

"Didn't you understand," he said, "all those hours that I sat for you while you painted, and these long nights in which we wandered by the water?"

"I thought you were my friend."

"I thought so too. When I sat before you and watched you paint, and looked at your beautiful hair and your eyes, I thought I was your friend. And I looked at the lines of your body beneath your dress. And when it pleased me to carry your easel and walk with you, I thought it was friendship. Only tonight I know I am in love. Oh, Valentia, I am so glad!"

She could not keep back her tears. Her bosom heaved, and she wept.

"You are a woman," he said. "Did you not see?"

"I am so sorry," she said, her voice all broken. "I thought we were such good friends. I was so happy. And now you have spoilt it all."

"Valentia, I love you."

"I thought our friendship was so good and pure. And I felt so strong in it. It seemed to me so beautiful...."

"Oh, Valentia, don't leave me. I can't—I can't live without you."

She heard the unhappiness in his voice. She turned to him again and laid her two hands on his shoulders.

"Why can't you forget it all, and let us be good

friends again? Forget that you are a man. A woman can remain with a man for ever, and always be content to walk and read and talk with him, and never think of anything else. Can you forget it, Ferdinand? You will make me so happy."

He did not answer, and for a long time they stood on the bridge in silence. At last he sighed—a heartbroken sigh.

"Perhaps you're right. It may be better to pretend that we are friends. If you like, we will forget all this."

Her heart was too full; she could not answer; but she held out her hands to him. He took them in his own, and, bending down, kissed them.

Then they walked home, side by side, without speaking.

Such a one do I remember, whom to
look at was to love.

—*Alfred, Lord Tennyson*

But there's nothing half so sweet in life
As love's young dream.

—*Thomas Moore*

To die for one you love,
'tis but an easy task!
And I am filled with exaltation.
I am invaded with new force,
I go where love calls me.

—*Gluck (from an opera called* Aleceste*)*

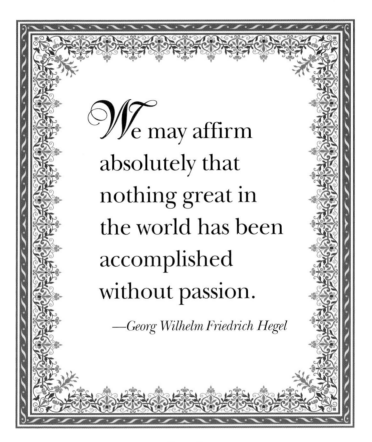

We may affirm
absolutely that
nothing great in
the world has been
accomplished
without passion.

—*Georg Wilhelm Friedrich Hegel*

In courtesy I'd have her chiefly learned;
Hearts are not had as a gift but hearts
 are earned.

—*William Butler Yeats*

Let's contend no more, Love,
Strive nor weep:
All be as before, Love,
—Only sleep!

—*Robert Browning*

Do Not Trifle with Love

—*Alfred de Musser*

Tis strange what a man may do, and a woman yet think him an angel.

—*William Makepeace Thackeray*

Love is that condition in which the happiness of another person is essential to your own.

—*Robert A. Heinlein*

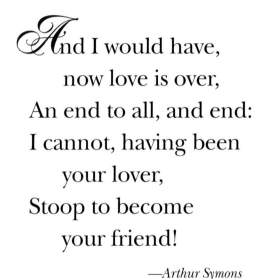

And I would have,
    now love is over,
An end to all, and end:
I cannot, having been
    your lover,
Stoop to become
    your friend!

—*Arthur Symons*

*O*ne human Being, entirely loving me
would not only have satisfied all my
Hopes, but would have rendered me
happy and grateful, even tho' I had had
no Friend on earth, herself excepted.

In short, a WIFE, in the purest,
holiest sense of the word.

—*Samuel Taylor Coleridge*

*I*t is best to love wisely, no doubt;
but to love foolishly is better than not
to be able to love at all.

—*William Makepeace Thackeray*

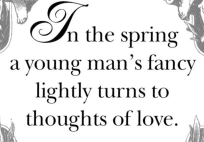

*I*n the spring
a young man's fancy
lightly turns to
thoughts of love.

—*Alfred, Lord Tennyson*

*B*ehold, you are fair, my love!
Behold, you are fair!
You have dove's eyes behind your veil.
Your hair is like a flock of goats,
Going down from Mount Gilead.
Your teeth are like a flock of shorn sheep
Which have come up from the washing,
Every one of which bears twins,
And none is barren among them.
Your lips are like a strand of scarlet,
And your mouth is lovely.
Your temples behind your veil
Are like a piece of pomegranate.
Your neck is like the tower of David,
Built for an armory,
On which hang a thousand bucklers,
All shields of mighty men.
Your two breasts are like two fawns,

Twins of a gazelle,
Which feed among the lilies.

You have ravished my heart,
My sister, my spouse;
You have ravished my heart
With one look of your eyes,
With one link of your necklace.
How fair is your love,
My sister, my spouse!
How much better than wine is your love,
And the scent of your perfumes
Than all spices!
Your lips, O my spouse,
Drip as the honeycomb;
Honey and milk are under your tongue;
And the fragrance of your garments
Is like the fragrance of Lebanon.

—*Song of Solomon, 4:1–5; 9–11 (NKJV)*

*H*e will hold thee, when his passion
shall have spent its novel force,
Something better than his dog,
a little dearer than his horse.

—*Alfred, Lord Tennyson*

*T*o have known love,
how bitter a thing it is.

—*Algernon Charles Swinburne*

*T*o live is like to love—all reason is
against it, and all healthy instinct for it.

—*Samuel Butler*

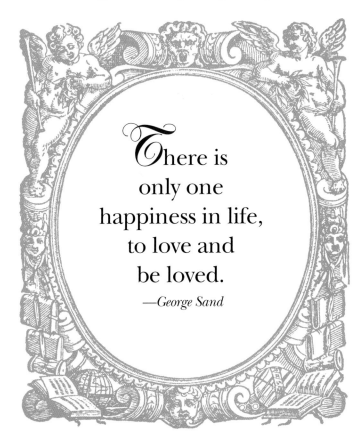

There is
only one
happiness in life,
to love and
be loved.

—*George Sand*

I have lived long enough, having seen one thing, that love hath an end.

—*Algernon Charles Swinburne*

Love is...born with the pleasure of looking at each other, it is fed with the necessity of seeing each other, it is concluded with the impossibility of separations!

—*José Martí*

I hold this to be the highest task of a bond between two people: that each should stand guard over the solitude of the other. For, if it lies in the nature of indifference and of the crowd to recognize no solitude, then love and friendship are there for the purpose of continually providing the opportunity for solitude. And only those are the true sharings which rhythmically interrupt periods of deep isolation.

—*Rainer Maria Rilke*

*N*o human creature can give
orders to love.

—*George Sand*

*O*ur heart is a treasury; if you
spend all its wealth at once you are
ruined. We find it as difficult to
forgive a person for displaying his
feeling in all its nakedness as we
do to forgive a man for being
penniless.

—*Honoré de Balzac*

*O*h to love so, be so loved, yet so
mistaken!

—*Robert Browning*

*O*ut of my thoughts! You are part of my existence, part of myself. You have been in every line I have ever read, since I first came here, the rough common boy whose poor heart you wounded even then. You have been in every prospect I have ever seen since—on the river, on the sails of the ships, on the marshes, in the clouds, in the light, in the darkness, in the wind, in the woods, in the sea, in the streets. You have been the embodiment of every graceful fancy that my mind has ever become acquainted with. The stones of which the strongest London buildings are made, are not more real, or more impossible to be displaced by your hands, than your presence and influence have been to me, there and everywhere, and will be. Estella, to the last hour of my life, you cannot choose but remain part of my character, part of the little good in me, part of the evil. But, in this separation I associate you only with the good, and I will faithfully hold you to that always, for you must have done me far more good than harm, let me feel now what sharp distress I may. O God bless you, God forgive you!

—*Charles Dickens,* Great Expectations

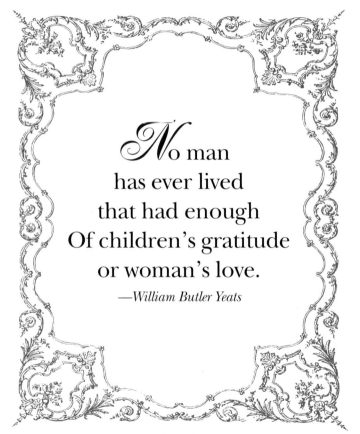

*N*o man
has ever lived
that had enough
Of children's gratitude
or woman's love.

—*William Butler Yeats*

*L*ove is, above all, the gift of oneself.

—*Jean Anouilh*

*T*here is a smile of love,
And there is a smile of deceit,
And there is a smile of smiles
In which these two smiles meet.

—*William Blake*

*T*he fundamental error of their matrimonial union; that of having based a permanent contract on a temporary feeling.

—*Thomas Hardy*

Hell, Madame, is to love no longer.

—*Georges Bernanos*

Over the mountains and over the waves,
Under the fountains and under the graves;
Under floods that are deepest, which
    Neptune obey,
Over rocks that are steepest, Love will find
    out the way.

—*Anonymous*

THE PLEASURE-PILGRIM

by Ella D'Arcy

She made him all sorts of silent advances, speaking with her eyes, her sad little mouth, her beseeching attitude. And then one evening she went further still. It occurred after dinner in the little green drawing room. The rest of the company were gathered together in the big drawing room beyond. The small room has deep embrasures to the windows. Each embrasure holds two old faded green velvet sofas in black oaken frames, and an oaken oblong table stands between them. Campbell had flung himself down on one of these sofas in the corner nearest the window. Miss Thayer,

passing through the room, saw him, and sat
down opposite. She leaned her elbows on
the table, the laces of her sleeves falling
away from her round white arms, and
clasped her hands.

"Mr. Campbell, tell me, what have I
done? How have I vexed you? You have
hardly spoken two words to me all day. You
always try to avoid me." And when he began

to utter evasive banalities, she stopped him with an imploring "Ah, don't! I love you. You know I love you. I love you so much I can't bear you to put me off with mere phrases."

Campbell admired the well-simulated passion in her voice, and laughed aloud.

"Oh, you may laugh," she said, "but I'm serious. I love you, I love you with my whole soul." She slipped round the end of the table and came close beside him. His first impulse was to rise; then he resigned himself to stay. But it was not so much resignation that was required as self-mastery, cool-headedness. Her close proximity, her fragrance, those wonderful eyes raised so beseechingly to his, made his heart beat.

*L*et men tremble
to win the hand of woman,
unless they win along with it
the utmost passion
of her heart.

—*Nathaniel Hawthorne*

$\mathcal{L}$ove is and was my lord and king.

—*Alfred, Lord Tennyson*

$\mathcal{Y}$ea, kiss me one strong kiss of your heart,
Do not kiss more; I love you with my lips,
My eyes and heart, your love is in my blood,
I shall die merely if you hold to me.

— *Algernon Charles Swinburne*

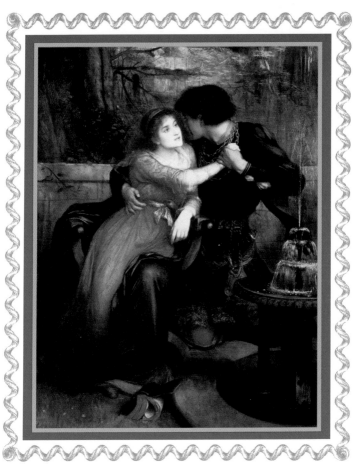

He had a dark face, with stern features and a heavy brow; his eyes and gathered eyebrows looked ireful and thwarted just now; he was past youth, but had not reached middle-age; perhaps he might be thirty-five. I felt no fear of him, and but little shyness. Had he been a handsome, heroic-looking young gentleman, I should not have dared to stand thus questioning him against his will, and offering my services unasked.

I had hardly ever seen a handsome youth; never in my life spoken to one. I had a theoretical reverence and homage for beauty, elegance, gallantry, fascination; but had I met those qualities incarnate in masculine shape, I should have known instinctively that they neither had nor could have sympathy with anything in me, and should have shunned them as one would fire, lightning, or anything else that is bright but antipathetic.

—*Charlotte Brontë*

I love those who yearn for the impossible.

—*Johann Wolfgang von Goethe*

If you love me as I love you,
What knife can cut our love in two?

—*Rudyard Kipling*

If you loved only what were
worth your love,
Love were clear gain,
and wholly well for you.

—*Robert Browning*

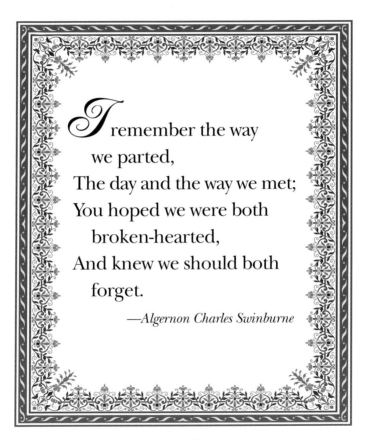

I remember the way
    we parted,
The day and the way we met;
You hoped we were both
    broken-hearted,
And knew we should both
    forget.

—*Algernon Charles Swinburne*

She is coming, my own, my sweet;
Were it ever so airy a tread,
My heart would hear her and beat,
Were it earth in an earth bed;
My dust would hear her and beat,
Had I lain for a century dead;
Would start and tremble under her feet,
And blossom in purple and red.

—*Alfred, Lord Tennyson*

Whoever has loved knows all that life
contains of sorrow and of joy.

—*George Sand*

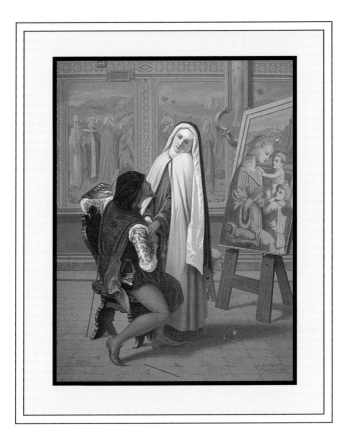

Love
To Faults
Is Always
Blind

$\mathcal{L}$ove to faults is always blind,
Always is to joy inclin'd,
Lawless, wing'd and unconfin'd,
And breaks all chains from every mind.

—*William Blake*

Whatever our souls are made of,
his and mine are the same.

—*Emily Brontë*

Escape me?
Never Beloved!
While I am I, and you are you.

—*Robert Browning*

Love seeketh not itself
    to please,
Nor for itself hath any care,
But for another gives its ease,
And builds a Heaven in
    Hell's despair.

—*William Blake*

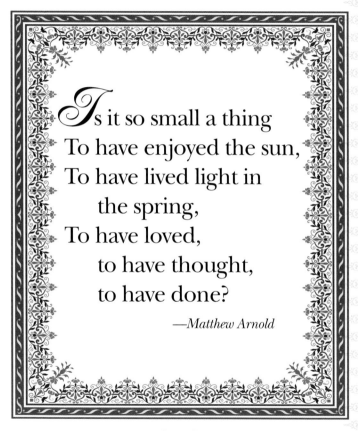

*I*s it so small a thing
To have enjoyed the sun,
To have lived light in
the spring,
To have loved,
to have thought,
to have done?

—*Matthew Arnold*

We cannot kindle when we will
The fire that in the heart resides,
The spirit bloweth and is still,
In mystery our soul abides.

—*Matthew Arnold*

How many loved your moments of glad grace,
And loved your beauty with love false or true,
But one man loved the pilgrim soul in you,
And loved the sorrows of your changing face.

—*William Butler Yeats*

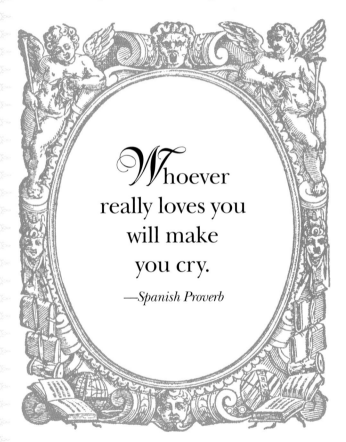

$\mathscr{W}$hoever
really loves you
will make
you cry.

—*Spanish Proverb*

Many will love you; you were made for love;
For the soft plumage of the unruffled dove
Is not so soft as your caressing eyes,
You will love many; for the winds that veer
Are not more prone to shift their compass, dear,
Than your quick fancy flies.

Many will love you; but I may not, no;
Even though your smile sets all my life aglow,
And at your fairness all my senses ache.
You will love many; but not me, my dear,
Who have no gift to give you but a tear
Sweet for you sweetness' sake.

—Mathilde Blind

*A*ll thoughts, all passions, all delights,
Whatever stirs this mortal frame,
All are but ministers of Love,
And feed his sacred flame.

—*Samuel Taylor Coleridge*

OUR NEIGHBOR, MR. GIBSON

by Florence Henniker

$\mathcal{S}$he was sitting, still dressed by the window, her head bent down over her knees. On a table in front of her was a folded letter, and a case in which I recognized the brooch shaped like a heartsease, shining under the candle. She turned her tear-stricken face to mine. My heart was very sore, as I knelt down by my poor child.

"Darling," I said, "*do*, do try not to think of him still."

"How *dare* you say that, father? I *know* he wasn't tired of me! Something—something else kept him away. Oh! father darling," and she fixed her passionate, sad eyes on me with a terrible earnestness; "I've sometimes thought it as *my* fault. There may have been that in his past life which he did not like to tell me. He thought me hard and narrow-minded. I've worried and worried myself till I felt almost mad sometimes, thinking that perhaps it was my want of sympathy that came between us. And yet he *must* have known how I cared! how I worshiped him!"

She flung her arms on the table, and I saw the hot tears running down between her fingers on to the ground.

Presently she raised her head.

"Father, do you think if I wait—and I am always, *always* waiting, we shall hear of him before long? He might come, mightn't he, when we least expect it?"

How could I resist the pleading agony in her voice? If I spoke, on the impulse of the moment, untruthfully, God forgive me!

"Yes, yes, my darling, it's quite possible. We may, of course, have news of him some day; good news!"

But, in my inmost heart, I know that we never shall.

*A*ll his faults are such that one loves him still the better for them.

—*Oliver Goldsmith*

The look of love alarms
Because 'tis fill'd with fire;
But the look of soft deceit,
Shall win the lover's hire.

—*William Blake*

Yet each man kill the thing
    he loves,
By each let this be heard,
Some do it with a bitter look,
Some with a flattering word
The coward does it with a kiss,
The brave man with a sword!

—*Oscar Wilde*

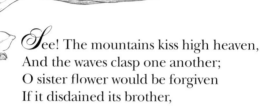

See! The mountains kiss high heaven,
And the waves clasp one another;
O sister flower would be forgiven
If it disdained its brother,

And the sunlight clasps the earth,
And the moonbeams kiss the sea;—
What are all these kissings worth,
If thou kiss not me?

—*Percy Bysshe Shelley*

I only know we loved in vain;
I only feel—farewell! farewell!

—*Lord Byron*

Such ever
was love's way:
to rise, it stoops.

—*Robert Browning*

It's Love That Makes The World Go Round!

Faint heart never won fair lady!
Nothing venture, nothing win—
Blood is thick, but water's thin—
In for a penny, in for a pound—
It's Love that makes the world go round!

—*Sir William S. Gilbert*

The joy of life is variety; the tenderest
love requires to be rekindled by intervals
of absence.

—*Samuel Johnson*

*N*one shall part us from each other,
One if life and death are we:
All in all to one another—
I to thee and thou to me!
Thou the tree and I the flower—
Thou the idol; I the throng—
Thou the day and I the hour—
Thou the singer; I the song!

—*Sir William S. Gilbert*

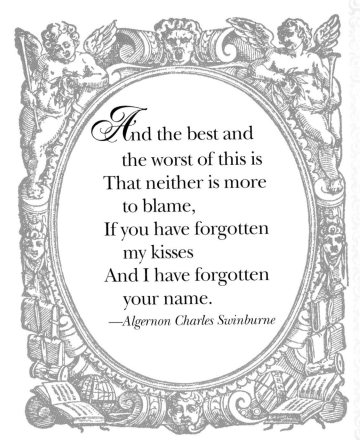

And the best and
the worst of this is
That neither is more
to blame,
If you have forgotten
my kisses
And I have forgotten
your name.

—*Algernon Charles Swinburne*

AN UGLY LITTLE WOMAN

by Nora Vynne

There is something in great agony that in itself strengthens us to endurance, but who can endure contempt? In the past she had been wounded and crushed, now every touch was agony, and no one spared her, why should they? What graces had she that should win tenderness, a little faded ugly woman, a mark for the mirth of the young and thoughtless, the

dislike of the sensuous, the impatience of the
strong? Nothing left her but patience, and
she had grown so very weary of patience. Life
would have been easier if she could have
been angry, but she had no cause for anger.
The world loves beauty, and youth, and happi-
ness, and she was old, and sad, and ugly.

The world was full of love, but not for her.
The world lives on hope, and she was hope-
less; the world is very beautiful, and she was a
stain upon it.

"Oh God! to be a woman, and old, and
ugly."

It broke his heart, the pain was too great
to be borne, he cried out aloud, and started
in his seat.

The little brown-faced woman at the further
end of the carriage started too, and shrank into
herself; he stared at her, bewildered.

It was so tragic, the gentle pathos of her

face, as if she would beg forgiveness for her very existence; as if she would cry out to him not to crush her, as insects are crushed by the strong because they are unsightly.…

Her pride touched him more than all, it was so impotent, so gentle. He moved along the seat till he was opposite her, looking straight into the patient, proud, pathetic face; he spoke tenderly, gently, and with infinite reverence.…

"Do you mind telling me where you are going now?"

"I am going be a drudge among strangers. What is it to you?"

What did it mean that he, a man in the prime of life, handsome, rich, overburdened with friends, felt the tears rise in his eyes, and a great ache in his heart? She might well look at him in wonder. He stretched out his hands towards her, he could scarcely speak.

"I have felt it all. You have suffered so much, you shall not suffer any more. I will make your life so bright to you if you will let me."

"I don't understand," she faltered.

"Neither do I," he cried, "neither do I, not how I know so much, or why I love you. I only know that I must take you right into my heart and keep you warm there, for I do love you!"

"Oh no! me, impossible!"

But looking in his eyes she saw that it was possible, and true, and she held out her hands, trembling, wondering, questioning. He answered the question with words that seemed to come through him, as if they were a message, and not only his own thought.

"Every human soul is lovable; we could not hold back from loving every soul on earth, could we once see it. But we cannot. Beauty hides the soul equally with deformity. Today God has been very good to me: I have seen the soul of a woman and loved it."

To suffer woes which Hope thinks infinite;
To forgive wrongs darker than death or night;
To defy Power, which seems omnipotent;
To love, and bear; to hope till Hope creates
From its own wreck the thing it contemplates;
Neither to change, nor falter, nor repent;
This, like thy glory, Titan, is to be
Good, great and joyous, beautiful and free;
This is alone Life, Joy, Empire, and Victory.

—*Percy Bysshe Shelley*

Though earth and man were gone,
And suns and universes ceased to be,
And thou wert left alone,
Every existence would exist in Thee.

—*Emily Brontë*

I am not a famous or even an
infamous man, but I have had a love
affair with my only wife, in sunshine
and showers, from the day when
I first saw her twenty-eight years ago.

—*Reverend Edward John Hardy,
dedication,* The Love Affairs
of Some Famous Men

Two Souls
With But
A Single
Thought

Two souls with but a single thought,
Two hearts that beat as one.

—*Friedrich Halm*

*S*he was a phantom of delight
When first she gleamed upon my sight;
A lovely apparition, sent
To be a moment's ornament.

—*William Wordsworth*

*T*hou shalt love and be loved by, for-
ever: a Hand like this hand
Shall throw open the gates of new life to
thee! See the Christ stand!

—*Robert Browning*

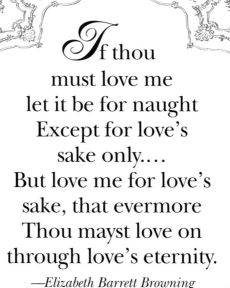

*I*f thou
must love me
let it be for naught
Except for love's
sake only....
But love me for love's
sake, that evermore
Thou mayst love on
through love's eternity.

—*Elizabeth Barrett Browning*

Ah, love, let us be true
To one another! for the world, which seems
To lie before us like a land of dreams,
So various, so beautiful, so new,
Hath really neither joy, nor love, nor light,
Nor certitude, nor peace, nor help for pain;
And we are here as on a darkling plain
Swept with confused alarms of struggle and flight,
Where ignorant armies clash by night.

—*Matthew Arnold*

IN A FAR-OFF WORLD
by Olive Schreiner

There is a world in one of the far-off stars, and things do not happen here as they happen there.

In that world were a man and woman; they had one work, and they walked together side by side on many days, and were friends.

But there was something in that star world that there is not here. There was a thick wood where the summer sun never shone; there stood a shrine. In the day all was quiet, but at night, when the stars shone or the moon glinted on the tree-tops, if one crept here quite alone and knelt on the steps of the stone altar, and uncovering one's breast, so wounded it that the blood fell down on the altar steps, then whatever he who knelt there wished for was granted.

Now, the man and woman walked together; and the woman wished well to the man. One night when the moon was shining so that the leaves of all the trees glinted, the woman walked alone to the forest. It was dark there; the moonlight fell only in little flecks on the dead leaves under her feet, and branches were knotted tight overhead. Farther in it got darker, not even a fleck of moonlight shone. Then she came to the shrine; she knelt down before it and prayed; there came no answer. Then she uncovered her breast; with a sharp two-edged stone that lay there she wounded it. The drops dripped slowly down on to the stone, and a voice cried, "What do you seek?"

She answered, "There is a man; I hold him nearer than anything. I would give him the best of all blessings."

The voice said, "What is it?"

The girl said, "I know not, but that which is most good for him I wish him to have."

The voice said, "Your prayer is answered; he shall have it."

Then she stood up. She covered her breast and held the garment tight upon it with her hand, and ran out of the forest. She ran along the smooth shore, then suddenly she stood still. Out across the water there was something moving. It was a boat; it was sliding swiftly over the moonlit water out to sea. One stood upright in it; the face the moonlight did not show, but the figure she knew. Faster and faster it glided over the water away, away. She ran along the shore; she came no nearer it.

Then a voice beside her whispered, "What is it?"

She cried, "With my blood I bought the best of all gifts for him. I have come to bring it him! He is going from me!"

The voice whispered softly, "Your prayer was answered. It has been given him."

She cried, "What is it?"

The voice answered, "It is that he might leave you."

The girl stood still.

Far out at sea the boat was lost to sight beyond the moonlight sheen.

The voice spoke softly, "Art thou contented?"

She said, "I am contented."

At her feet the waves broke in long ripples softly on the shore.

*G*row old along with me!
The best is yet to be,
The last of life for which the first was made:
Our times are in His hand
Who saith, "A whole I planned,
Youth shows but half; trust God;
    see all nor be afraid!"

—*Robert Browning*

*A*h Love! Could you and I with Him conspire
To grasp this Sorry Scheme of Things entire,
Would not we shatter it to bits—and then
Remold it nearer to the Heart's Desire!

—*Edward FitzGerald*

"Here, indeed, is the true lover," said the Nightingale. "What I sing of, he suffers: what is joy to me, to him is pain. Surely love is a wonderful thing. It is more precious than emeralds, and dearer than fine opals. Pearls and pomegranates cannot buy it, nor is it set forth in the market place. It may not be purchased of the merchants, nor can it be weighed out in the balance for gold.

—*Oscar Wilde,*
   The Nightingale and the Rose

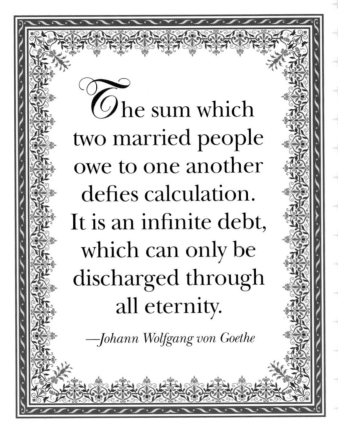

The sum which two married people owe to one another defies calculation. It is an infinite debt, which can only be discharged through all eternity.

—*Johann Wolfgang von Goethe*

O love, what hours were thine and mine,
In lands of palm and southern pine.

—*Alfred, Lord Tennyson*

*S*o long as the world contains us both,
Me the loving and you the loth,
While the one eludes, must the other pursue.

—*Robert Browning*

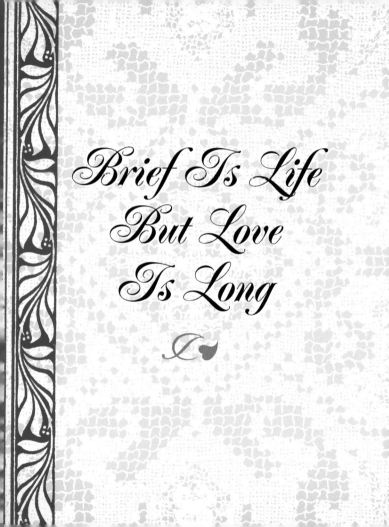

Brief Is Life
But Love
Is Long

O tell her, brief is life but love is long.

—*Alfred, Lord Tennyson*

*O*nly I discern
Infinite passion, and the pain
of finite hearts that yearn.

—*Elizabeth Barrett Browning*

*L*ove, like Death,
Levels all ranks, and lays the shepherd's
    crook
Beside the scepter.

—*Edward Bulwer-Lytton*

*A*h Christ, that it were possible
For one short hour to see
The souls we loved, that they might
    tell us
What and where they be.

—*Alfred, Lord Tennyson*

*H*ere are
fruits, flowers,
leaves and branches,
And here is my
heart which beats
only for you.

—*Paul Verlaine*

*T*hou wast that all to me, love,
For which my soul did pine—
A green isle in the sea, love,
A fountain and a shrine,
All weathered with fairy fruits and flowers,
And all the flowers were mine.

—*Edgar Allen Poe*

*N*ever give all the heart, for love
Will hardly seem worth thinking of
To passionate women if it seem
Certain, and they never dream
That it fades out from kiss to kiss;
For everything that's lovely is
But a brief, dreamy kind delight.

—*William Butler Yeats*

AN OLD WIFE'S TALE

by Ellen T. Fowler

———

"Tell me your love story, please," I coaxed
Mr. Weatherley.

"Oh! that is an old story, Ethel, a very
old story."

"I do *so* want to hear it," I urged.

"Then, I will tell it to you with pleasure.
When I was very young I met two most
charming orphan sisters, Naomi and Rachel
Lestrange. Naomi, the elder, was a quiet,
unobtrusive woman, with nothing distinctive
about either her character or her appear-
ance; but Rachel was the most beautiful and
lovable creature I ever saw in my life."

"I daresay," he continued, "that now it is

difficult for you to realize how very lovely my wife was when she was young. I have never seen her since, so she is still beautiful Rachel Lestrange to me; but I suppose her pretty hair is gray, and her dear face aged now."

"Well, of course I fell over head and ears in love with Rachel as soon as I set eyes on her. I have been in that state ever since. But before I dared to ask her to be my wife, the great catastrophe of my life occurred."

"What was that?"

"One bitter winter's night the Lestranges' house caught fire, and was burnt to the ground. When I appeared on the scene the two sisters were standing at their bedroom window shrieking for help."

"How terrible!" I exclaimed.

"I placed a ladder against the wall of the burning house, and ascended it; though already the walls scorched my hands, and the smoke was so dense that I could hardly see. I seized Rachel—who happened to be nearest to the window—in my arms, and carried her down the ladder. Then I reascended the ladder to save Naomi; but, alas! ere I was halfway up, the side of the house fell in, and I was precipitated into the burning ruins. Poor Naomi, of course, perished in the flames; but I was saved, though as by a miracle."

"When at last I did recover, it was to the sad consciousness that I should be hopelessly blind to the end of my life."

"How sad!" I whispered.

"Through all that long illness my Rachel nursed me and it was to her care that I really owed my recovery. Her name was ever on my lips, and I told her over and over again the story of my love for her.

"And when you were well enough, she told you the story of her love for you, I suppose."

"She did, bless her! she did. Rachel brought me away from the scene of our great catastrophe: there we were quietly married, and thence we sailed for England as soon as I was strong enough for the voyage."

"Poor Mrs. Weatherley! Did she feel her sister's death very much?" I asked.

"Sadly, my dear, sadly! In fact, I do not think she has ever been the same woman since. They were the most devoted pair of sisters I ever saw; but, I used to think that Naomi was just a little hard and severe on my sweet, loving Rachel."

"That is very likely," I said, "for I think it is quite impossible for those cold, calm natures to enter into the feelings of so passionately loving a woman as Mrs. Weatherley."

"But Rachel was always so utterly unselfish—as you see she is now in all her dealings with me—that she would rather suffer herself to any extent than let suffering fall on those whom she loved."

"It seems to me that Mrs. Weatherley has a perfect genius for loving," I said softly.

Within a few months of our conversation, Fortunatus Weatherly was dead; he died holding his wife's hand, and the last word he said was "Rachel."

One day, when she was very old indeed, Mrs. Weatherley said to me—

"I cannot forgive myself for letting Fortunatus save me, and leave my poor sister to be burnt to death."

"If she had lived and you had died, think what a difference it would have made to your husband!"

"I know, I have often thought of that, and it is my one comfort. Even had they married each other (which is doubtful, as my sister had a great horror of anyone with a physical infirmity), she could never have loved and cared for Fortunatus as I have done; it wasn't in her. My sister loved him then because she always adored strength and beauty; but she would not have had the patience to wait on a blind man all her life, which to me was perfect bliss," continued the old lady.

"He could not have lived without you, Mrs. Weatherly. Believe me, it is all for the best. I am sure that Naomi herself would forgive you, and understand."

She looked at me with sorrowful eyes. "I am Naomi," she said; "but he never found out."

They are not long, the weeping and the laughter,
Love and desire and hate:
I think they have no portion in us after
We pass the gate.

They are not long, the days of wine and roses;
Out of a misty dream
Our path emerges for a while, then closes
Within a dream.

—*Ernest Dowson*

*B*etter by far you should forget and smile
Than that you should remember and be sad.

—*Christina Rossetti*

*L*ife in common among people who
love each other is the ideal of happiness.

—*George Sand*

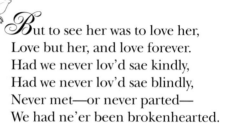

*B*ut to see her was to love her,
Love but her, and love forever.
Had we never lov'd sae kindly,
Had we never lov'd sae blindly,
Never met—or never parted—
We had ne'er been brokenhearted.

—*Robert Burns*

*L*ove is enough: though the world
be a—waning,
And the woods have no voice but the
voice of complaining.

—*William Morris*

I hold it true,
    whate'er befall;
I feel it when I
    sorrow most;
'Tis better to have
    loved and lost
Than never to have
    loved at all.

—*Alfred, Lord Tennyson*

ACKNOWLEDGMENTS

Artwork on cover and pages 2, 3, 12, 20, 38, 42, 43, 59, 72, 84, 87, and 125 from Wood River Media, San Rafael, California; Pages 7, 26, 57, 121, and 123: Courtesy of Robert Frederick, Ltd.; Pages 18, 33, 45, 47, 53, 56, 63, 75, 76, 81, 88, 90, 93, 96, and 114 courtesy of Library of Congress, Verner W. Clapp Fund; Pages 21 and 103: "Spring Flowers" by Currier & Ives; Page 23: The Huguenot" by Sir John Everett Millais (1829-1896) Robert Frederick, Ltd.; Page 51: "The Love Letter" by John William Godward (1861-1922) Robert Frederick, Ltd.; Page 65: "Romeo and Juliet" by Henri Pierre Picou (1824-1895) Robert Frederick, Ltd.; "The Lovers Reconciliation" by Currier & Ives; Page 100: "Miranda—The Tempest" by John William Waterhouse (1849-1917) Robert Frederick, Ltd.; Page 104: "The Marriage" by Currier & Ives; Page 108: "Will She?" by Mary Ellen Staples. Haynes Fine Art Gallery, Broadway, Great Britain. Fine Art Photographic Library, London/Art Resource, NY; Page 111: "The Lovers' Picnic" by Auguste Hadamard (1823-1886), Fine Art Photographic Library, London/Art Resource, NY.